WORD TRAVELERS
TRAVELERS
AND THE
BIG CHASE IN PARIS

THE
WORD TRAVELERS
SERIES

WORD TRAVELERS
AND THE BIG CHASE IN PARIS

RAJ HALDAR
ILLUSTRATED BY **BEATRIZ CASTRO**

sourcebooks
eXplore

For Devika, the newest little word nerd in our family.

Published by Sourcebooks eXplore, an imprint of Sourcebooks Kids
P.O. Box 4410, Naperville, Illinois 60567-4410
(630) 961-3900
sourcebookskids.com

Cataloging-in-Publication Data is on file with the Library of Congress.

Source of Production: Sheridan Books, Chelsea, MI, United States
Date of Production: August 2023
Trade Paperback ISBN: 9781728271088 Run Number: 5030726
Hardcover ISBN: 9781728271071 Run Number: 5030725

Printed and bound in the United States of America.
SB 10 9 8 7 6 5 4 3 2 1

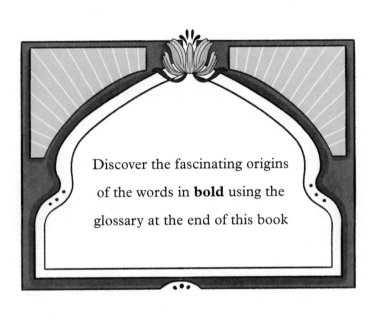

Discover the fascinating origins

of the words in **bold** using the

glossary at the end of this book

Welcome to **France**

The Journal Newspaper

The Pompidou Center

Luxor Cinema
Palace

Eiffel Tower

River Seine Art Walk

a of the Sacred Heart

ARIS

Train to Nice

re Museum

acombs of Paris

NICE

THE KNIFE
AND
STICK CAFÉ

Knife and Stick Café

N
W   E
S

1

COSTUME CONFIDENTIAL

Eddie had been looking forward to this day for the whole month of April. It was still winter when his mom signed the permission slip for Ms. Cassatt's yearly trip to the city art museum. Now, on this crisp spring morning, the school bus packed full of fourth and fifth graders had finally arrived. The old yellow bus screeched to a stop as a high-pitched voice came over the loudspeaker.

"OK, my little *artistes*. The time has come for us to put on our imagination caps!" said a crackly voice.

Molly-Jean spotted her best friend, Eddie, and ran down the aisle to grab the seat next to him. "Ms. Cassatt does this every year," MJ explained excitedly. "She hands out special hats for all the kids to wear at the art museum."

Eddie looked up and saw Ms. Cassatt digging around in her giant orange handbag. As usual, her outfit was a dazzling explosion of color: a flowing yellow dress with huge blue earrings in the shape of two triangles. Sitting on top of her curly red hair was a purple **beret**—a brimless kind of hat that artists wore back in the old days. *You can tell that Ms. Cassatt is an art teacher just by looking at her*, Eddie thought to himself.

"I think we have to get creative and change our plans!" Ms. Cassatt's voice came booming out of the bus's loudspeaker once again. She had a frazzled look on her face. "I left the box of berets back at the school. So we will be wearing *pretend* hats for the class trip today."

MJ made a motion to adjust her make-believe beret. "Oh well," she shrugged. "I guess that's why they call it an 'imagination cap!'" With that, Eddie, MJ, and the rest of the kids lined up in the aisle, laughing and giggling as they stepped down the stairs at the front of the bus.

"Whoa!" Eddie shouted as he laid eyes on at the massive set of stairs leading up to the art museum for the very first time.

3

"There must be hundreds of people sitting on these steps," he said, nudging MJ.

"There's a juggler and even a jazz band playing too," MJ replied, pointing out the performers who had come to entertain all of the visitors at the world-famous museum. While the two friends were busy looking around, MJ noticed that their classmates had already lined up in front of the big doors at the museum's entrance. "Last one to the top of the stairs is a rotten..." But before she could finish her sentence, Eddie had already taken off like a rocket, climbing the museum steps. "Hey! Wait for me," cried MJ as she followed in hot pursuit.

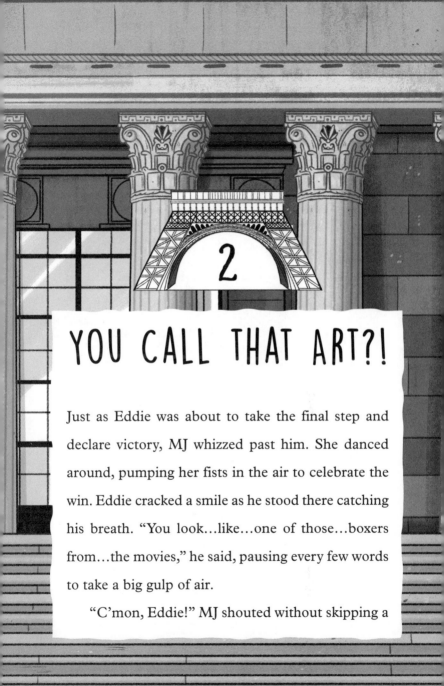

2

YOU CALL THAT ART?!

Just as Eddie was about to take the final step and declare victory, MJ whizzed past him. She danced around, pumping her fists in the air to celebrate the win. Eddie cracked a smile as he stood there catching his breath. "You look...like...one of those...boxers from...the movies," he said, pausing every few words to take a big gulp of air.

"C'mon, Eddie!" MJ shouted without skipping a

beat. "Ms. Cassatt's museum tour is starting now." The two friends joined the rest of the class as everyone filed in through the big double doors. They gathered in front of the information stand at the center of the museum's gigantic entrance hall.

"The special exhibit should be through that door on the left!" shouted Ms. Cassatt, holding up a map of the museum's three floors. But Eddie noticed something silly. He pushed his way through the crowd of kids and nudged his teacher's hand.

"Um, Ms. Cassatt?" Eddie whispered. "I think we need to go the other way. You're holding the map upside down!"

"Holy pretzel! So I am," she exclaimed. Everyone knew Ms. Cassatt could be a little scatterbrained, but she was the best art teacher anyone ever had. "Ahem. The exhibit we've all come to see is just through those doors *on the right*," she corrected herself. But only half the students heard her. A big group of fifth-grade boys headed in one direction. Some younger

kids went the other way. A few other confused students stood in the center of the entrance hall scratching their heads.

Ms. Cassatt peered down at Eddie with a worried look on her face. "Oh dear," she cried. "What in the world are we going to do now?"

"Can I see that map, Ms. C?" Eddie replied. She nodded and handed the paper to him. Without even looking down at it, Eddie rolled the map into a cone shape and put it to his lips.

"Attention, Ms. Cassatt's class! Listen up," Eddie shouted. With the help of his homemade megaphone, Eddie's voice boomed and echoed around the huge room. "Please meet through the door at the far right of the entrance hall. You'll see a big sign that says, *Modern Art Gallery*." Just like that, kids from every corner of the entrance hall flocked toward the area of the museum where the special exhibit was being held.

"Phew! Thanks, Eddie," said Ms. Cassatt.

Inside the gallery, crowds of children were bouncing from one kooky piece of art to the next. MJ saw her classmate Zane standing in front of a giant blue **canvas**. "You call that art?!" he exclaimed. "Even I could color in a whole piece of paper with blue **crayon**. It's easy!"

Ms. Cassatt grinned at Zane knowingly. "For hundreds of years, people only painted pictures of royal families and scenes from important books and…"

"…bowls of fruit!" Eddie said with a guffaw.

"Exactly," Ms. Cassatt continued. "When the modern artists came along, they decided to change the whole idea of what art could be in the first place."

"That blue…" MJ said, taking a second look at the canvas. "It's exquisite!"

Just then, Eddie shouted over to MJ. "What in the world is this?" He was sitting on a bench up close to a big painting with lots of colors.

MJ scooched next to her pal with a perplexed look on her face. "It's just a bunch of dots," she said.

As the two kids sat there looking at the strange work of art, they heard their teacher's voice coming from behind them. "Well, you're right and wrong all at the same time," Ms. Cassatt said. "Why don't you try taking ten steps backward? Slowly."

Eddie and MJ stood up and started counting with each step.

"ONE. TWO. THREE. FOUR..."

When Eddie and MJ were standing farther away from the painting, a picture slowly began to appear.

"Whoa! Do you see that, MJ?" Eddie said excitedly. "There are a bunch of people in the painting."

"I can see a guy with a pointy hat, I think!" MJ replied.

"FIVE. SIX. SEVEN. EIGHT..."

After they took four more steps back, the drawing became even clearer. "There's a tent and a crowd of people watching something," Eddie whispered.

"Amazing," said MJ. "Just two more steps."

"NINE... TEN."

From halfway across the gallery, MJ and Eddie could finally see the painting clear as day. It was an old-timey scene. People were gathered in front of a circus tent. Inside, a clown wearing a pointy hat was performing. There was a band playing music in the background. MJ turned around to Ms. Cassatt. "It's like magic, Ms. C!"

"Sort of," she said with a wink. "It's the magic of *pointillism*."

"Pointy what?" Eddie asked.

"You're telling us that drawing pointy hats is a special kind of art?" MJ asked.

"Point-il-lism," Ms. Cassatt repeated the word slowly, letting out a hearty laugh. "It's a style of art that uses tiny little dots to make a picture that can only be seen from far away. It works by tricking our brains into blending those little dots together when we look at the painting from…"

Ms. Cassatt was suddenly interrupted by a loud commotion from the far end of the gallery. A group of students had gathered around something, but MJ couldn't make out what it was. The kids were hooting and hollering. "Right in the middle of the gallery here?" she heard someone shout.

"I can't believe it," said one of the fourth grade girls.

Eddie, MJ, and Ms. Cassatt made their way over

to the other end of the room, and finally they saw what all the commotion was about. Eddie and MJ could hardly believe their eyes.

They heard their friend Zane shout, "Now I've seen everything! That's not art. It's just a regular old **toilet**!"

Everyone laughed. Eddie stood on his tippy-toes to get a better look. There really was a toilet just sitting right there in the middle of the modern art gallery with red velvet ropes around it.

MJ ran over to the little white label on the wall to learn more about the precious potty. She read out loud: "This ordinary toilet was submitted to the museum 100 years ago to show that even everyday objects could be seen as beautiful pieces of art. Since then, it has become one of the most famous pieces of modern art in the world, proving that art is truly all around us."

"That's right, MJ," Ms. Cassatt chimed in. "The artist even gave this regular old toilet a very impressive name."

"What is it?" Eddie asked, eyes wide with excitement.

"It's called *The Fountain*," said Ms. Cassatt.

The whole class giggled. "Yuck! Like the water fountains we have back at school?" they heard a kid from the crowd ask.

Ms. Cassatt paused to think. "How about the beautiful water sculptures you find inside parks?" she replied.

MJ turned to Eddie and whispered. "Well, which version is true? Where did the word *fountain* even come from?" she wondered aloud. "Maybe we should look it up. Tell me you remembered the Awesome Enchanted Book..."

Eddie smiled at MJ and reached inside his backpack, "You think I'd forget our magical book on this special class trip to the city art museum?!" Just like that, out came their trusty AEB, the old book handed down to Eddie by his great-grandpa Oscar. Even though the AEB had almost all the words in the English language listed from A to Z, it wasn't like any old dictionary. You see, Eddie's great-grandfather was a famous *etymologist*—someone who studies how all sorts of common words come to our language from cultures around the world. Great-Grandpa Oscar spent his whole life collecting words we use every day and discovering the amazing stories of how we started using them in the first place! He then recorded his findings in the book.

MJ quietly grabbed the AEB and untied the shoelaces that held the massive book together. The golden globe and silver swirls of alphabet letters that were stamped on the cover started to glow. The other kids were too busy laughing about the toilet to notice what the two friends were up to. MJ flipped through the pages and found the section for the letter F. "Let's see here," she said, brushing her finger along the words on each page. "Farmhouse. Fascinating. Feather…"

"There!" Eddie whispered, pointing down at the opposite page. He read the entry aloud. "Fountain comes from the Old French word *fontaine*, which means 'spring of water that collects in a pool.'"

MJ and Eddie looked over at the precious potty and back at each other with excitement. "I guess a toilet can be a fountain. It's all about how you look at things," said MJ.

Suddenly, the AEB left their hands and started spinning in the air like it had a mind of its own.

Then, without warning, they heard a loud flushing sound coming from the toilet, and before they knew it, the whole gallery started spinning, taking MJ and Eddie with it.

"I'm starting to get really dizzy!" Eddie shouted.

"Here we go! It's like **déjà vu** all over again," replied MJ, knowing that an incredible adventure was about to begin.

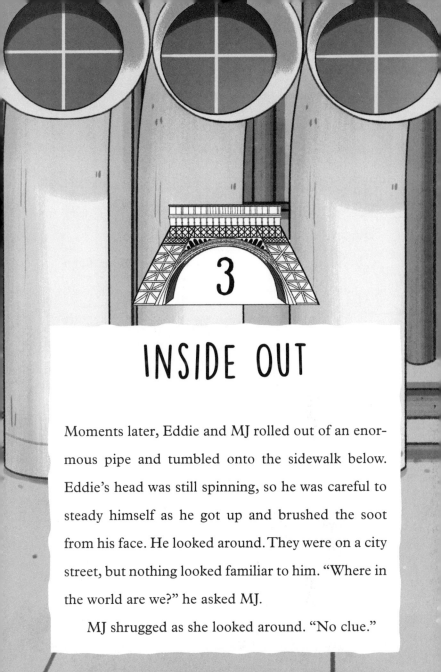

3

INSIDE OUT

Moments later, Eddie and MJ rolled out of an enormous pipe and tumbled onto the sidewalk below. Eddie's head was still spinning, so he was careful to steady himself as he got up and brushed the soot from his face. He looked around. They were on a city street, but nothing looked familiar to him. "Where in the world are we?" he asked MJ.

MJ shrugged as she looked around. "No clue."

Eddie peered out at the bustling city and saw a river snaking through its center. "Lots of cities are built around bodies of water," he explained. "We learned that in second grade geography." MJ could tell that Eddie was stumped because his face was all scrunched up in a funny way.

Suddenly, MJ gasped. "Look at the skyline! I can see the most famous tower in the whole world."

"You don't mean?" Eddie asked. "The Magnolia Street water tower back home, do ya?"

"No, *mon frère*—this is something way bigger. It's the Eiffel Tower," MJ replied excitedly.

"We're in Paris, France!" the two friends said at exactly the same time. Before they even had a second to catch their breath, MJ and Eddie noticed something else astonishing. There was a huge building standing above them, but it was unlike anything either of them had seen before. There were enormous pipes zigzagging all over the outside of the strange building.

"Usually they hide all those pipes *inside* the building," said Eddie. He thought for a second and then added, "It's like the whole thing is inside out!"

"Yeah! It almost looks like something out of a video game," MJ replied.

"Look," Eddie shouted, pointing up. As if things couldn't get weirder, the two friends saw a young boy about their age flipping and twirling across the exposed pipes, making his way down to the street. With a final triple backflip, the boy landed on his feet right next to MJ and Eddie. His bright green exercise jumpsuit with matching sneakers made the boy pretty hard to miss.

"A perfect ten!" said MJ with a smile on her face.

"You must be some kind of gymnastics champion," Eddie added.

The boy laughed as he pushed back his mop of curly brown hair and said, "Oh no, my friends. This is a kind of **sport** called parkour—where we turn the whole city around us into an obstacle course for our acrobatic tricks."

"It's almost like skateboarding..." MJ started.

"But without a skateboard," Eddie said, finishing his best friend's sentence. He stared back up at the tubes crisscrossing the building. "I couldn't think of a better place to practice your tricks either."

"This is our city's famous modern art museum, the Center Pompidou," replied the boy. Bringing up the museum must have reminded him of something, because MJ noticed a worried look on his face.

"Is everything OK with you...?" MJ trailed off, realizing she didn't even know the boy's name.

"My name is Sami," he said, putting two fingers up in a peace sign to wave hello. "It is my father's dream to display his art in the museums of this great city," Sami continued. "I came here to show them his newest painting," he said as he unrolled a small piece of canvas.

Eddie and MJ looked down and marveled at the spectacular piece of art. MJ instantly remembered her favorite part of Ms. Cassatt's class, when they looked at famous drawings and talked about what they liked about them. Sami's dad's art reminded her of the beautiful paintings by van Gogh, Picasso, and Frida Kahlo. "Your dad is a genius!" MJ said.

The young boy smiled. "Thank you for saying it. My father was a talented artist back in Egypt where he grew up. He went to the best art schools and then came here to Paris with the dream of becoming a world-famous painter." Sami carefully rolled up his father's painting and placed it under his arm. "The museum rejected his painting again." Sami frowned. "For now, Papa sells his art at a little stall down by the river."

At that very moment, a tall man wearing a uniform interrupted the three friends. "*Excusez-moi*!" he said, looking down over his round eyeglasses at Eddie, MJ, and Sami.

Eddie had heard that phrase a million times in the French movies he watched with his mom and dad. "That means, 'Excuse me,'" he whispered in MJ's ear.

"I know, silly!" she whispered back.

The man cleared his throat and continued. "Oh, you're just a bunch of kids," he said, looking relieved. "I thought I saw someone climbing around the outside of the museum," the gentleman continued. "You see, all of us museum guards have been on high alert ever since the rumors started going around that the Ballerina has returned."

"The Ballerina? Who's that?!" asked MJ.

The guard reached into his pocket and pulled out a page he ripped from a newspaper called the *Journal*. "Here!" he exclaimed. "There have been sightings of the famous art thief all over the city for the past two weeks."

MJ looked down and read from the article. "Despite the rumors, no one can be sure if she is really back or if she'll strike again."

"Check this out," said Eddie pointing to a few sentences from another article at the edge of the newspaper clipping. "This week, our paper received a mysterious message that we have yet to unscramble."

"So what's the clue?" asked Sami excitedly.

MJ looked down and began reading slowly:

*I'm not a **souvenir***
It soon will be clear
*When again I'm **on point***
And the chat disappears

"Oh goodness!" MJ sighed. "How can a person be a souvenir? It's just another word for something you buy from a museum gift shop, right?"

"I don't know, MJ," Eddie replied. "Maybe this is a job for the AEB." In a flash, he had their beloved book open to search all the words starting with S. "Aha! Here it is," shouted MJ. "*Souvenir* comes from an Old French word meaning *memory*."

"That makes perfect sense," added Sami. "You buy a souvenir from the gift shop to have a memory of your trip to the museum."

"Totally!" said Eddie, looking giddy as ever. "So the first part of the clue actually means, 'I'm not a *memory,*'" he pieced together.

"But what about this gobbledygook?" MJ asked, looking back at the scrap of newspaper. "What does on point mean here?"

"When you're dressed up all snazzy?" Eddie wondered.

MJ rolled her eyes and laughed. "You think you're so cool, Eddie." *But why do we even use that phrase in the first place?* she asked herself as she once again looked down at the AEB. She knew that their magic book didn't just have single words, but it also included common phrases. "There we go! *On point,*" she exclaimed.

Eddie read aloud. "Yep! 'On point. When someone is bold, excellent, or performs well,'" he started. But suddenly he was completely tongue-tied and couldn't get out any words.

"What is it?" Sami asked.

Finally, Eddie pulled himself together and continued reading. "It says here that the phrase may come from the French *en pointe*, a ballet term meaning 'to be on one's tippy-toes.'"

The three friends looked around at each other, completely astonished. She was no longer a memory of the past. The Ballerina had indeed returned!

"We have to go warn the editor of the *Journal* newspaper," Sami shouted as the three friends left sprinting down the street.

The Journal: News You Can Use

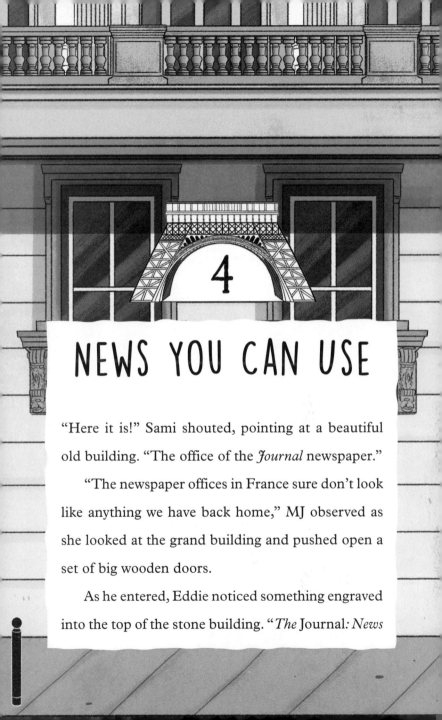

4

NEWS YOU CAN USE

"Here it is!" Sami shouted, pointing at a beautiful old building. "The office of the *Journal* newspaper."

"The newspaper offices in France sure don't look like anything we have back home," MJ observed as she looked at the grand building and pushed open a set of big wooden doors.

As he entered, Eddie noticed something engraved into the top of the stone building. "*The* Journal: *News*

You Can Use," Eddie read the words out loud. "That must be the newspaper's slogan."

Inside, Eddie, MJ, and Sami found themselves smack-dab in the middle of a busy newsroom. There were phones ringing and people shouting all around them. "This is a loud place to work," yelled MJ over the racket, but her friends couldn't hear.

"What's that?" a potbellied man with a **pencil** behind his ear stood up from his desk. "Are you *allowed* to work? Well, of course," he continued, mis-hearing what MJ had said. "I need you to get the scoop on this Ballerina stuff that everyone around Paris is whispering about!"

"But, but...we're not..." Eddie started to say.

"I'm your editor, Mr. Pierre. And I give out the assignments here!" he interrupted. Mr. Pierre looked around at everyone in the newsroom and shouted. "As a reminder, our newspaper's name, Journal, comes from the Old French word *jornel*, meaning a day's work. Not a week's work. Not a month's work.

So hop to it!"

MJ turned to Eddie and said, "I don't think we have a choice here."

Eddie nodded and looked up at Mr. Pierre. "Eddie and Molly-Jean, star **reporters** at your service. We've already cracked the clue in yesterday's newspaper, and it's true, the Ballerina has returned!"

But Mr. Pierre had already moved on. He yelled at another reporter across the room, "I need tomorrow's front-page story on my desk by noon. The Louvre Museum plans to reveal an incredible Egyptian statue called the Bastet Cat."

"I've heard of the Louvre," said MJ. "It's the famous museum in Paris where visitors can see the Mona Lisa and so many more priceless works of art."

"More people visit the Louvre every year than any other museum on earth!" Sami added excitedly.

Mr. Pierre looked up from his desk. "There's no time to waste. You must find out where the Ballerina will strike next." he ordered.

"OK! We'll file a report soon," said MJ, giving Mr. Pierre a salute as the three friends raced out of the newsroom.

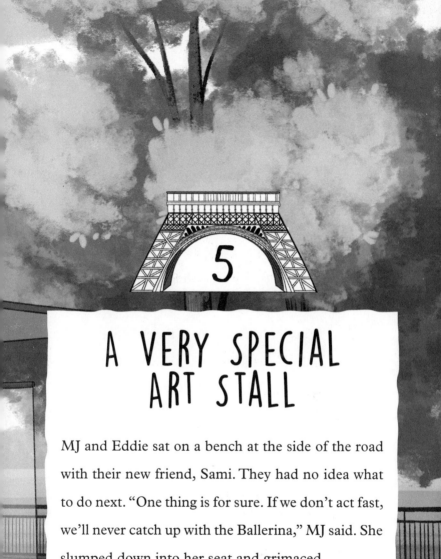

A VERY SPECIAL ART STALL

MJ and Eddie sat on a bench at the side of the road with their new friend, Sami. They had no idea what to do next. "One thing is for sure. If we don't act fast, we'll never catch up with the Ballerina," MJ said. She slumped down into her seat and grimaced.

For a long while, no one said anything. After a few minutes, Sami shot up from the bench with a frantic look on his face. "We have to get back to Papa's art stall!" he announced. "He's waiting to hear if his painting was accepted to the museum's show," Sami said, wincing as he thought about having to share the bad news.

Just then, a city bus pulled to the side of the road next to the three kids. They hadn't realized it until that moment, but they were sitting at a bus stop!

Sami was a city kid, and he knew every bus route by heart. "This bus is **en route** to the river Seine," he shouted, and the friends jumped aboard. It was just a few stops to Sami's father's art stall along the river. When the kids got off the bus, they waved thanks to the driver. "*Au revoir!*"

"That means 'goodbye' in French," Sami said, winking at the others.

As the bus drove off behind them, MJ and Eddie looked around and couldn't believe their eyes. The sidewalk along the river was dotted with little stalls selling books, pieces of art, and more. "Which stall is

40

your dad's, Sami?" asked MJ. "There must be hundreds of them."

"This way," he replied. MJ and Eddie followed their friend, weaving through the crowds of tourists until they arrived.

Sami's father, Ali, sat in front of an easel at his stall, painting the scenery of Paris. Without looking up from his work, he said hopefully, "Sami, my boy! Will my painting be shown in the museum at long last?"

Sami looked down and kicked a small rock into the river. He thought for a minute, because it was hard to know how to break the bad news to his father. "Your painting wasn't accepted, Papa. I'm sorry."

Eddie felt so bad that he started to tear up. But then, Sami's dad looked up from his painting and smiled. "Well, there's always next time! Nothing worth getting ever comes easy," he said. It was only then that the older man noticed Eddie and MJ. "Who are your new friends?" he asked.

"They're the lead reporters hot on the trail of the Ballerina," Sami explained without skipping a beat.

Sami's father dropped his paintbrush on the ground. "She's...she's back?!" he stammered in a low voice.

MJ picked up the brush and handed it back. "Here you are, Mr. Ali," she said.

He smiled warmly at MJ and continued, "The Ballerina was on the prowl when I first arrived here in Paris from my home country of Egypt many years ago. As a young artist, I was saddened each time she looted another priceless work of art from our museums."

"Why do they call her the Ballerina anyway?" Eddie wondered.

"She dances across the rooftops of our fair city by night, using her incredible ballet skills to avoid being captured," Mr. Ali explained. "She is also a great lover of art. The Ballerina only steals the best works by the greatest masters."

Suddenly, the conversation was interrupted by a loud thud as several paintings from Mr. Ali's stall came crashing to the ground.

"*Le chat terrible!*" Sami's dad exclaimed in French.

"That means 'the terrible cat' in French," explained Sami.

"This stray black cat is very cute, but she's always knocking down my paintings," Mr. Ali said in a huff.

"Hang on," said Eddie, eyes wide with excitement. "*Chat* is French for *cat*? Why didn't you say so earlier?" He began doing a little dance and laughing hysterically.

"What is it, Eddie?" demanded MJ.

"Look at the last line of the clue from the newspaper," he said while continuing his little jig.

MJ pulled out the scrap of newspaper and read the last line again. "And the *chat* disappears." MJ was completely thunderstruck as it dawned on her as well. "You're brilliant, Eddie!" she said excitedly. "The Ballerina is saying that a cat will disappear."

The three friends shouted all at once, "the Bastet Cat!"

"Mr. Pierre, the editor of the newspaper, told us that the statue will be shown at the Louvre Museum in just one week's time!" MJ explained.

Mr. Ali stared at Eddie and MJ in disbelief. "One of the greatest artifacts of ancient Egypt could be lost forever," he said. "Many years ago, there were rumors that the Ballerina's favorite place to practice was at the highest point in all of Paris."

For a moment, everyone was quiet. But then, Eddie noticed Sami's eyes get as big as Ping-Pong

balls. "I know exactly where you mean," shouted Sami. Eddie and MJ weren't surprised that their new friend knew where to go next.

"Sami knows Paris like the back of his hand," Eddie said to MJ, but it was too late. She'd already darted off down the street, following their new friend.

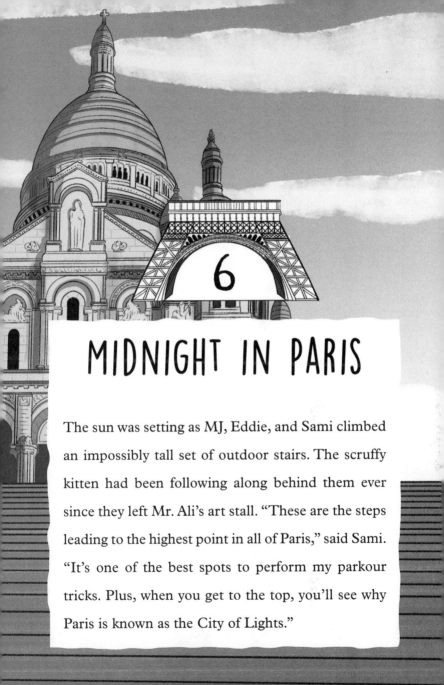

6

MIDNIGHT IN PARIS

The sun was setting as MJ, Eddie, and Sami climbed an impossibly tall set of outdoor stairs. The scruffy kitten had been following along behind them ever since they left Mr. Ali's art stall. "These are the steps leading to the highest point in all of Paris," said Sami. "It's one of the best spots to perform my parkour tricks. Plus, when you get to the top, you'll see why Paris is known as the City of Lights."

MJ took a deep breath as she began climbing up the mountain of steps. Before long, Eddie was getting very tired, so he started pulling himself up each step by holding on to the railing. Eddie had been counting the stairs from the very bottom, but he was so out of breath that he stopped saying the numbers out loud. When they reached the very last stair, Eddie laid down on the ground and sputtered, "Two hundred and twenty-two…"

"That's a lot of stairs," said MJ, who was crouching down to catch her breath. When she finally looked up, MJ was astonished by the **marvelous** view in front of her. The whole city of Paris was twinkling with light as far as her eyes could see. In the distance, MJ could even make out the Eiffel Tower. *I'm in love with this place*, she thought to herself.

Sami tapped MJ on the shoulder. "Look behind you," he whispered. She had been so focused on the beautiful view of the city that she didn't even notice the pretty church that sat on top of the hill behind them. It was all lit up so that the people of Paris could see it by night.

Suddenly, as Eddie was admiring the old church building, something flickered past his eyes. "Did you see something?" he whispered to his friends. "There it is again," he pointed.

"Whoa!" said MJ a few seconds later. "I think it was the shadow of a dancer," she gasped.

"The Ballerina! Her **silhouette** must be coming from that direction," Eddie pointed across the lawn in front of the church. The three friends sprinted through the darkness, but there was nobody there.

Once again, the shadow of the Ballerina appeared, looming large across the front of the church. This time she wasn't moving at all. "The Ballerina is playing with us now," Eddie whispered. "Where could she be?"

"There!" Sami pointed. MJ and Eddie looked over and saw something rustling in the bushes. They ran back in the other direction.

"There's no one here," MJ frowned.

"Maybe it was a squirrel scurrying around," Sami suggested. "But I could've sworn…"

Just then, Eddie stepped on something and almost tripped. He bent down to see what it was. "Guys, you're never going to believe this…" he said with amazement. The three friends gathered around and saw exactly what Eddie had walked into. Lying there on the ground was a ballet shoe.

MJ knelt on the ground and picked up the pink slipper. She turned it around in her hands and noticed two words written inside the sole of the shoe. She read them aloud:

Coupon Sabotage

"That's a funny name for a shoe company," Eddie joked.

"Stop being silly," MJ said sternly. "It's a clue from the Ballerina. But what could it mean?"

In an instant, Eddie pulled out the AEB and began flipping through the pages. "Let's see here," he said, rubbing his chin while he scanned the words starting with C. "Circle...Coach...Coupon!"

"Well, what does it say?" MJ asked impatiently.

"Coupon comes from the French word *couper*..."

Sami interrupted. "It means 'to cut' in our language!"

Eddie was gobsmacked. "That makes perfect sense. My mom loves cutting coupons out of the newspaper to bring to the grocery store."

But MJ had already grabbed the AEB and moved onto the second part of the clue. "Sabotage, sabotage, sabotage," she said as she scoured their trusty book.

"*Sabotage* means when you mess something up on purpose," said Eddie.

"Right!" MJ shouted as she looked down at the AEB. "It says here that *sabotage* was a way of saying, 'Walk noisily,' from the Old French word *sabot*, meaning 'shoe'!"

Without warning, the stray cat that had been following the kids all afternoon leapt up and snatched the shoe right out of Eddie's hands. She rolled around playing and clawing at the slipper.

"Stop it, you naughty kitty!" MJ shouted.

But it was too late. The kitten had already ripped the Ballerina's shoe to shreds and was lying on the ground purring with satisfaction.

"We're sunk," Eddie muttered. "Without this shoe, we're never going to find out where to go next."

MJ sat down just in front of the shredded ballet shoe. "You're right, Eddie. What're we supposed to do now?"

For a moment, it was so quiet that you could hear a pin drop. Suddenly, Sami started howling with laughter.

"What is it, Sami?!" Eddie asked incredulously. "What could possibly be funny at a time like this?"

Sami looked toward his friends as he finally put

the whole clue together. "*Coupon Sabotage*," he whispered and looked around. "The Ballerina is telling us to *cut the shoe*!"

"It's as if our little feline friend was trying to help us out," added MJ as she picked up the shredded slipper and examined it. There were pieces of cloth and paper strewn about everywhere. "When I was little, my mom put me in ballet classes. I remember these shoes have paper stuffed in the tip to make it easy to stand on your tippy-toes."

As MJ idly pulled the paper out of the "pointe" of the shoes, she discovered something incredible. "The toe of the Ballerina's slipper isn't just stuffed with any old scraps of paper," she said. "These are movie tickets!"

"Lemme see!" said Eddie impatiently. MJ passed the tickets to her friend, who held them up to the moonlight and read out loud.

Luxor Cinema Hall
Monday Matinee
11:00 o'clock

"Tomorrow is Monday!" MJ shouted.

"That's easy! *Matinee* is French for *morning*," Sami added. "We had better get back to my dad's house and rest up for our next dance with the Ballerina!"

MONDAY MATINEE

The very next morning, Sami's father prepared a hearty breakfast of eggs, pastries, and raspberry jam for the kids. Afterward, they waved goodbye, excited to continue their adventure hot on the trail of the Ballerina.

"Thank you, Mr. Ali!" MJ said, grabbing the AEB and stuffing it in their knapsack as they left.

Luckily, the movie theater was just a few short

blocks from Sami's house. As they walked, Eddie looked down at his trusty Swiss Army watch and realized it was already a quarter to eleven. "The Monday matinee starts in fifteen minutes," he reminded the others. "We'd better hustle!"

With that, Sami started running down the street, expertly hopping on and off benches and swinging from lampposts as he went. "His parkour skills are amazing," said MJ, as she and Eddie struggled to keep up. When they finally arrived at the theater, the two friends looked up in awe of something else entirely.

The old movie theater was nothing like the ones that they liked to visit back home. It was decked out with oodles of squiggly designs and even hieroglyphics that reminded MJ of ancient Egypt. Across the top of the theater was a big sign that read, *Luxor Cinema Palace*.

"Most people don't realize this, but movies didn't start out in Hollywood," said Sami. "I learned in school that the cinematograph—or *cinema* for short—was invented here in France, by the Lumière Brothers way back in the 1890s."

"That's exactly right!" said a teenage boy who was sitting in the box office booth selling movie tickets. "As you can see, we love our cinema halls here in

Paris," he continued. "Tickets, please. The matinee begins in just two minutes."

Eddie stuffed his hand into the pocket of his shorts and fished out the three tickets for the Monday matinee. "Here you go, sir!" he said dutifully, and the three kids scampered into the **foyer** of the grand movie theater.

"We still have one minute! Who's up for some buttery popcorn, hot dogs, and cheesy nachos?" Eddie shouted excitedly. But there was no concession stand serving food anywhere in sight.

"What gives?! Where's the food?" MJ asked, looking over at Sami.

"Here in France, we only eat before or after the movies, but never during," their friend explained, shaking his head. "Anyway, let's find our seats. The show is about to start."

MJ, Eddie, and Sami entered the dark theater and shuffled past the other moviegoers who were already seated in their row. "*Excusez-moi*! Pardon me," whispered MJ. They had hardly been in France for two days, and MJ was already picking up the language.

The kids sat down in three empty seats in the center of the cinema hall just as the movie started. Eddie sank down into his chair and relaxed. He always enjoyed watching old movies that came out way before he was born. It was interesting to see how people dressed and talked. The movie that was chosen for the Monday matinee couldn't have been more perfect—it was one of those comedy capers about a jewel thief, and it was in French too! MJ, on the other hand, was sitting on the edge of her seat, looking around the theater for any sign of the Ballerina. *Keep an eye out for her shadow on the movie screen*, she told herself.

For almost twenty minutes it went on like that. Eddie was laughing and shouting with excitement, completely wrapped up in the flick. Meanwhile, MJ kept her eyes peeled for the mysterious Ballerina.

Suddenly, the projector started to slow down, and all the voices sounded deep and warbly. The movie had gotten stuck! The other moviegoers began grumbling in their seats and demanding their money back. So nobody besides MJ noticed when the silhouette of the Ballerina danced across the screen for just a split second. "Did you see that?!" she said, nudging Eddie.

Then a voice came over the loudspeaker. "Um. Something has gone horribly wrong in the projection room," they said nervously. "Please be patient while we attempt to fix the problem."

"That sounds like the boy who was working at the ticket counter." Eddie guessed. "We have to help him!"

The threesome darted out of the theater and up the stairs into a small room the size of a closet.

"Oh, thank goodness!" said the teenage boy, seeing that help had arrived.

"What happened?" MJ asked.

"I'm not sure. I looked away for just a second, and suddenly the movie reel was overflowing out of the projector."

Eddie looked around and saw that the tiny room was filled up with an impossibly long strip of bendy plastic. "This is a movie?" he asked in disbelief, picking up a little segment of the film strip. Getting a better look, Eddie saw that it was just a series of still pictures put together in a sequence. "It's like a giant flip-book!"

"*Précisément!*" the boy exclaimed. "You're right!"

The three friends began feeding the film back into the projector. "It won't start going until we get every last bit back onto the reel," said the projectionist. The crowd below in the theater was getting angrier as the minutes ticked by. MJ worked furiously, as her mind wandered thinking about how projectors work.

"Wait!" she exclaimed in a flash of brilliance. "Maybe the Ballerina stopped the projector on a particular frame because she was trying to tell us something." She peeked through the little window that looked out onto the theater. The movie was stuck on a frame showing the jewel thief speaking to a young lady at a beachside **restaurant**."

Eddie read the English subtitles that translated the movie at the bottom of the screen:

I know a Nice café. The omelets and baguettes are wonderful.

MJ's eyes lit up. "It's a clue," she whispered.

Eddie slumped down on a rickety wooden chair in the dusty projection room. "If the Ballerina is trying to tell us something, she sure has a funny way of doing it," he sighed.

But MJ noticed something else. "There's something strange about that sentence. See it?" The others looked at the caption again but couldn't find anything amiss. "The word *'Nice'* is capitalized," she continued. "Why would that word be capitalized in the middle of a sentence unless..."

Eddie finished MJ's thought. "Unless it's a proper noun, like a person or a place!"

The teenage projectionist, who had been listening in the whole time, stood up and shouted, "Nice! It's a city in the south of France. The name is pronounced the way you say the English word *niece*," he explained.

"But there must be hundreds of cafés that serve omelets in Nice," replied Sami.

"Omelet, omelet, omelet," MJ repeated. "It's a strange word when you think about it," she said. "Where on Earth did it come from?!"

Without thinking twice, Eddie pulled out the AEB and flipped to the page with words starting with O. "Here it is," he said and read the entry out loud. "Omelet comes from the Old French word *alemele* meaning 'knife blade.'"

"Incredible! Because of its flat shape," MJ figured.

"What's a bag-u-ette?" Eddie asked, trying to sound out the word.

MJ smiled. She was only a year and a half older than her little friend, but she loved to teach him new things. "It's one of those long rolls of bread that your dad always eats his turkey sandwiches on!" she said.

"I can help with that one," Sami said. "*Baguette* translates to 'stick' in English, because of its long thin shape."

"Knife and Stick Café!" the projectionist shouted. "It's the name of the most famous beachside café in all of Nice."

Just then, Sami pushed the last of the film onto the reel, and the projector came humming back to life.

"How can I ever thank you?" the boy cried.

"We're the ones who should be thanking you for all your help!" MJ shouted as the three kids bounded out of the movie palace and into the midday sun.

8

ALL ABOARD!

Before they knew it, Eddie, MJ, and Sami were aboard the overnight train heading for the city of Nice. The conductor came through their car to welcome the young travelers. He handed them dinner menus, pillows, and the late edition of the *Journal* newspaper.

"*En voiture!*" the conductor shouted.

"All aboard, as you say in English," Sami offered,

and the train began chugging along away from the station.

For the first time since their adventure began, MJ had a moment to take a deep breath and relax. When she looked down, however, something very interesting caught her eye. There was a newspaper article about an art auction happening at the Knife and Stick Café the very next day. According to the late-breaking story, many rich and famous people from around the world would be in attendance.

"The Raffles Brothers?!" Eddie shouted, reading the article over MJ's shoulder.

"What are you talking about, Eddie?" MJ asked.

Eddie squinted his eyes. "Don't you remember Geoffrey and Edgar Raffles from our adventure in India? They had their slimy paws on our friend's treasure so they could turn a school into a shopping mall, the scoundrels!"

"Of course I do," MJ replied. "But why on earth are you bringing them up now?" she asked.

"Look," Eddie said, pointing down at the paper. There was a picture of two mischievous men with matching curlicue moustaches.

MJ read the words below the photo aloud. "The wealthy Raffles Brothers hope to acquire the Egyptian Bastet Cat statue. The artifact would enter their vast private collection after being shown to the public for the last time at the Louvre Museum on Friday."

"Wait," Eddie started. "So you're telling me that even if we *do* somehow catch the Ballerina, the Bastet Cat might still be lost forever to those dastardly Raffles Brothers."

"And there's nothing we can do about it!" added MJ.

MJ leaned her head on the train window, taking in the scenery. As the sun went down, the big city gave way to small towns and beautiful rolling hills. Ordinarily, she would have been thrilled about an overnight train journey. But instead, she was feeling utterly hopeless as she dozed off.

9

A NICE PLACE TO VISIT

When MJ opened her eyes, it was already morning. "I must've been really tired," she told the others. "Where are we?"

A bell rang repeatedly as the train slowed to a stop. "We've finally arrived in Nice!" Sami replied. Eddie had already packed up everyone's bags and was standing in the aisle ready to get going!

Sometimes a good night's sleep is all you need, MJ thought to herself, feeling energized and totally refreshed.

The conductor passed through the car and smiled down at the kids. "Enjoy your stay in Nice. It's a nice place to visit!" he said, letting out a laugh.

Stepping out of the train station, Eddie and MJ instantly understood why so many people loved to go on vacation in Nice. There were beautiful beaches as far as the eye could see. Fancy hotels and restaurants dotted the coastline, and the whole place was buzzing with tourists.

"I didn't even bring my snorkel!" Eddie frowned. For a moment, he forgot all about the task at hand and began walking toward the sandy beach.

"There's no time for relaxing," said MJ. "We've got to get to the Knife and Stick Café pronto and stop the Raffles Brothers!"

"There." Sami pointed at a bustling **restaurant** a few blocks in front of them.

Eddie couldn't quite read the sign, but he saw the symbol of a sword and stick crossing each other in the shape of an X. "The Knife and Stick Café," he shouted.

The three friends sprinted down the street. When they finally arrived in front of the restaurant, they could see through the window that the auction had already begun.

"I hope we're not too late," MJ said as she opened the door for the others.

Inside, the Knife and Stick Café was filled with people hoping to bid more money than anyone else and win their favorite items.

A snooty old man stood in front of a podium at the front of the restaurant. He looked down over his round glasses at a piece of paper. "The next item for auction today is the incredible Bastet Cat statue," he read. "This cat sculpture dates back to ancient Egypt and was only rediscovered in the back room of the Louvre Museum just a few months ago. All of the money raised in the sale of this artifact will go toward building the museum's new wing."

A hush fell over the crowd. It was the moment everyone had been waiting for. MJ scanned the room and noticed two sketchy-looking men sitting at the front of the restaurant. "The Raffles Brothers!" she shouted.

"Shhh!" said Eddie, putting his pointer finger up to his lips. But it was too late.

Geoffrey Raffles turned around and spied MJ and Eddie. "Curses!" he said, whispering something into his brother Edgar's ear.

"Two hundred. Do I have two hundred? OK!" the auctioneer began speaking rapidly. "Three hundred. Come get the Bastet Cat for just three hundred bills. Any takers?!"

The Raffles Brothers raised a **plaque** with their name on it each time, and the price went up and up.

"The auctioneer sure has a funny way of talking," Sami noticed.

It went on like this for a few minutes, and the number just kept soaring higher until there were only two bidders left—the Raffles Brothers and an old lady sitting in the back of the restaurant.

"One thousand, folks. Come and get your kitty cat. For the princely sum of ten thousand euros, you too can own a piece of Ancient Egypt!" the auctioneer proclaimed.

Out of nowhere, Sami raised his hand. "What're you doing?" MJ warned. "We don't have that kind of money. We're only kids!"

But from the smirk on his friend's face, Eddie could tell that Sami had a trick up his sleeve. "I'll take the Bastet Cat..." he said loudly.

The auctioneer raised his gavel. "Going once.

Going twice..."

"For five bucks, because it looks like a fake!" Sami shouted, just to cause a commotion. All at once, everyone in the audience gasped.

Knock! Knock! Knock!

"Please calm down," the auctioneer pleaded while banging his gavel. "The item being auctioned is not a **counterfeit**," he assured the group. But it was already too late. During the ruckus, the old lady in the back row who was bidding against the Raffles Brothers slipped off her curly gray wig, revealing her long **brunette** hair.

"She's not a granny at all," Eddie shouted. The surprised look on his face was priceless.

"It's...it's..." Sami stammered. "It's the Ballerina!"

"Thanks, kids!" the Ballerina said with a devious smile. Then, before anyone had a chance to act, she began twirling her whole body around in a ballet move called a *pirouette*. Gaining speed as she spun

like a top, the Ballerina launched herself across the room in the longest ballet jump anyone had ever seen.

Ooh! Ahh! Ohh!

Everyone in the crowd was dazzled by the **marvelous** dancing. Everyone except the Raffles Brothers, that is!

"Edgar! Fetch the golden **receipt** from the auctioneer, and the Bastet Cat will be ours," Geoffrey commanded his younger brother. Edgar leapt into action, sprinting toward the auctioneer's desk. At that exact moment, the Ballerina landed just next to the podium, but she was a hair too late.

"No!" shouted Eddie and MJ, watching as Edgar Raffles grabbed the golden receipt and slid away through the crowded restaurant.

"Follow that man!" said MJ, looking back toward the Ballerina. But the cunning cat burglar had disappeared too.

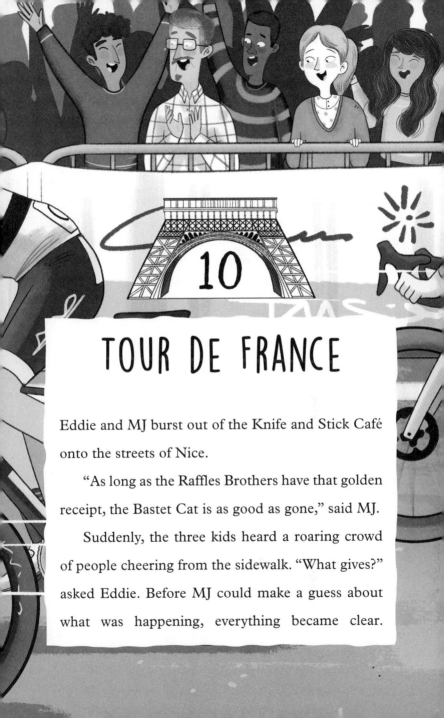

10

TOUR DE FRANCE

Eddie and MJ burst out of the Knife and Stick Café onto the streets of Nice.

"As long as the Raffles Brothers have that golden receipt, the Bastet Cat is as good as gone," said MJ.

Suddenly, the three kids heard a roaring crowd of people cheering from the sidewalk. "What gives?" asked Eddie. Before MJ could make a guess about what was happening, everything became clear.

Hundreds of bicyclists started whizzing down the street past the three friends.

"The Tour de France!" exclaimed Sami. "The world-famous bike race that goes through much of our beautiful country is happening right now!"

"And we're right in the middle of it," MJ observed.

"Friends," Sami said, pointing toward the sea of bicyclists passing by. "The Raffles Brothers are getting away!"

MJ couldn't believe her eyes. Geoffrey and Edgar Raffles were racing off into the sunset riding a tandem bicycle—the kind with two sets of pedals and two seats.

"They'll have twice the power with that thing!" Eddie figured.

Before they knew what was happening, MJ and Eddie had somehow walked into an area where competitors in the great bike race were getting ready. A coach squeezed water from a bottle into Eddie's mouth. "Um, thanks!" he said, water dribbling down his cheek. Eddie, MJ, and Sami were each given their own bikes and matching helmets.

"Go! Go! Go!" the crowd roared.

And like that, the three friends gave chase, competing in the world-famous Tour de France bike race. MJ squinted looking into the blinding sun ahead of her and could barely make out the Raffles Brothers off in the distance. "We have to really put the pedal to the metal," she said.

The trio began pedaling faster than they ever had before. Little by little, they closed in on the Raffles Brothers. Along the way, the landscape around them changed from craggy cliffs looking over the beautiful blue sea to fields of yellow and gold flowers everywhere.

"There's no time to stop and smell the roses," Sami said. He kicked his right pedal down and pulled up on the handlebars. Sami's bike did a wild wheelie, and he started moving faster and faster. The Raffles Brothers weren't far off now.

Eddie saw a piece of **debris** on the street ahead. "Let's use it as a ramp!" he suggested.

"Are you sure?!" shouted MJ nervously, as the trio lined up their bikes one behind the other. Like pinballs, they catapulted through the air one by one, sailing over the competitors that had been in front of them and landing safely just next to the Raffles Brothers.

"Yes!" Sami rejoiced, raising his fist in the air.

But the Raffles Brothers wouldn't be beaten that easily. "Hit the brakes!" Edgar shouted to Geoffrey. "Our **chauffeur** is just around this corner." Before they knew it, the Raffles Brothers had pulled their tandem bicycle over behind a bush and hopped into a car that had been waiting for them all along.

"See you at the finish line, suckers!" Geoffrey

sneered at MJ and Eddie as their driver sped away.

Cheaters never win, MJ said to herself. She was so mad at the Raffles Brothers that it gave her a burst of energy. MJ shot up a steep mountain pass faster than everyone else.

"It's up to you now!" Sami shouted from behind as MJ pulled away from her friends.

The race had taken them all the way from the coast to a hilly area near the Alps mountain range. MJ passed the other competitors until she was in second place. Up ahead, she spied the Raffles Brothers at the side of the road. They were getting back on their tandem bike and pretending they rode it the whole way. MJ pulled up next to the brothers.

"Looks like my little **detour** worked!" Geoffrey cackled as they came to the last downhill leg of the race.

MJ could see the finish line up ahead. The two began gaining speed down the hill. For a few seconds, MJ inched in front of the Raffles Brothers, and in the

next moment, they would pull ahead. Suddenly MJ heard a loud bang. The Raffles's tire had popped, and his back wheel began skidding all over the place. MJ tried to slow herself down to catch them, but she was too late. Her bike was careening toward the finish line as she took second place in the Tour de France almost by accident!

The audience erupted into a thunderous roar as MJ was practically blinded by the flashes from all the cameras. For a moment, she enjoyed her big win by doing a little dance in the street. But then she remembered that the Raffles Brothers had disappeared, along with any chance of saving the priceless Bastet Cat.

Coming down the finish line with the middle of the pack, Eddie and Sami congratulated MJ on her second-place win. "Boy, am I happy to see you guys!" MJ said.

"Can I look at your medal?" Eddie asked.

"This is for all of us," MJ said, putting the silver

medal around her little buddy's neck. Eddie turned the medal around in his hands, beaming with pride. As he did, the young boy noticed something strange engraved on the back.

"It's a message," he said, taking a deep breath. "From the Ballerina!"

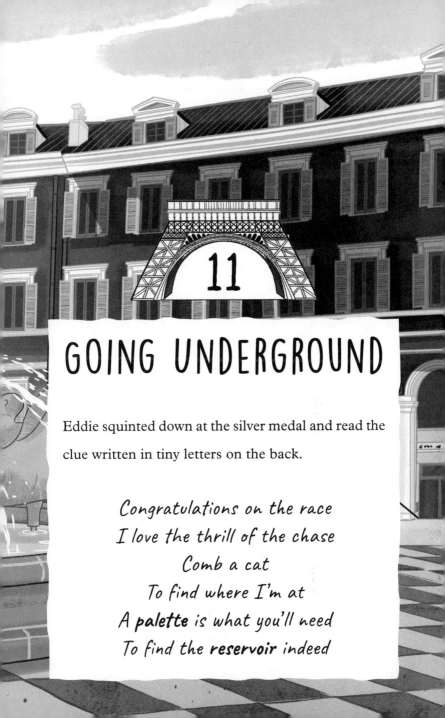

11

GOING UNDERGROUND

Eddie squinted down at the silver medal and read the clue written in tiny letters on the back.

Congratulations on the race
I love the thrill of the chase
Comb a cat
To find where I'm at
*A **palette** is what you'll need*
*To find the **reservoir** indeed*

"Just a bunch of gibberish as usual," MJ sighed. "The Ballerina is toying with us."

"She just wants to have us follow along so she can outsmart us," Sami agreed. "What's the point?"

There adventure had already been full of so many ups and downs. But this time the gang really felt hopeless. The Ballerina was always one step ahead of them. Besides, the Raffles Brothers had the golden receipt. No matter what happened, the Bastet Cat was going to end up in the wrong hands.

By this time, the hubbub from the Tour de France was over, and the fans had all gone home. The finish line was a ghost town, and it had become eerily quiet. MJ sat down to rest.

Sami mumbled something, breaking the silence.

"What'd you say?" MJ asked.

"Palette isn't just an art word," he repeated. "I mean it's not just the thing where you put your paints. It can also mean 'a small shovel' in French." Sami repeated the sentence from the clue. "A palette is what you'll need."

"What do we need a small shovel for?" MJ asked incredulously.

"There's only one thing to do with a shovel, MJ," Eddie replied.

"Dig underground!" the three friends said at once.

They looked back at the rest of the message from the Ballerina. "The last line says that we have to find a reservoir," Sami pointed out.

MJ knew from her family hiking trips that a reservoir was a big lake where drinking water came from. "Now the Ballerina is going to have us digging around for some underground lake?" she said. "Throw me the AEB, Eddie!" She flipped to the R section and quickly found the word. "Here," she said, reading the entry closely. "The original meaning of **reservoir** in French is just a storehouse."

"So we're not just looking for a lake," Sami replied.

MJ kept reading. "A place where something tends to collect, where anything is stored."

"OK, so we're looking for something kept underground. But where?" Eddie said as he looked down at the clue. MJ noticed her friend's eyes squinting. He always did that when he was concentrating really, really hard. "Comb a cat...comb a cat..." Eddie kept repeating to himself. "Maybe a long-haired cat would need a comb..."

Suddenly, Sami flipped in the air with joy, doing one of his acrobatic parkour tricks. "That's it!" he shouted.

MJ and Eddie were totally confused.

"'Comb a cat' backwards is *cat-a-comb*," Sami said the word slowly, looking up at his friends. "It's another word for an underground tomb."

"Creep-tastic!" Eddie laughed, doing a little zombie dance with his arms stretched out in front of him.

Sami smiled and continued in a hushed tone. "Underneath the city of Paris there is a gigantic maze of catacombs."

MJ's eyes grew wide as she put it together. "The Ballerina is luring us back to Paris," she said to the others. "We have to get on the next train. There's no time to lose!"

"But why is the Ballerina leaving a trail for us to follow her at all?" Eddie asked.

"Because she loves the thrill of the chase," Sami grinned as the three friends took off on their bikes to catch the next train back to Paris.

COMB A CAT?!

After a long train journey and several stops on the **Metro**—Paris's famous underground subway—Eddie, MJ, and Sami finally arrived at the entrance to the Catacombs.

"The sign says we can't go in. It's another dead end," Eddie sighed.

"That's just an old sign from when these underground tunnels were still being used," Sami explained. "Now it's been turned into a museum. See?" he said, pointing toward a tour guide speaking to a group of visitors.

"*Mesdames et messieurs*! Ladies and gentlemen. The tour of the historic catacombs of Paris begins now. Please follow me!" the tour guide said as she directed the tourists down a long flight of stairs.

"Why don't we tag along?" MJ whispered. The three friends blended in perfectly with the tour group, which included grown-ups and kids from all over the world.

As they walked down the stairs, Eddie and MJ started counting like they always liked to do. Just when Eddie thought they couldn't go down any further, the winding steps just kept going and going. Finally they arrived. "One hundred and thirty-one steps!" Eddie exclaimed.

"That's a long way down," MJ added as they entered a gigantic underground hall. Her voice echoed around the massive room.

"It sure is!" exclaimed the tour guide. "We are more than five stories underneath the streets of Paris," she offered. "Originally, these tunnels were dug out for mining rocks in ancient times. It wasn't until the Middle Ages that the catacombs started being used as…"

The guide stopped and pointed her flashlight at the wall for the first time.

MJ was speechless. The walls were stacked from end to end with skulls. Not only that, the old bones were stacked into different patterns.

"As a cemetery," the tour guide finished her sentence after pausing to build up excitement.

"This place is giving me the heebie-jeebies," Eddie admitted, turning to walk back up the stairs they had just come down.

MJ grabbed her best friend, Eddie, by his backpack. "C'mon! This is exactly the kind of thing you like in those goofy old adventure movies," she said. Then, something truly incredible caught her eye.

"Anyway, I have a feeling we're getting very close to the Ballerina. Look! This must be where she practices her moves," MJ said with a grin.

In a dark corner of the room, there was a huge mirror with a long bar for practicing ballet, and a pink **leotard**, the kind of exercise outfit worn by ballet dancers, MJ, Eddie, and Sami stepped away from the tour group and tiptoed over to the article of clothing.

"Did you know that the leotard is actually named after a person?" Sami explained as they made their way across the cavernous room.

"Really?!" said MJ incredulously.

Sami nodded his head. "It's true. The stretchy outfit gets its name from Jules Léotard, the man who invented the flying trapeze!"

"Whoa! That's so cool," said Eddie. He had heard the word *leotard* many times but had never once thought about what it actually meant. As they chatted, the three friends had wandered off from the

109

rest of the tour and suddenly found themselves alone in a dark room. Eddie heard something. "Was that you, MJ?" he asked.

"What're you talking about? I didn't say anything," MJ started. But then she heard it too. It was the voice of a woman.

"The **cashier** needs a **pen**!"

The words bounced all around the room. "The Ballerina!" Eddie exclaimed. "She's right here in the catacombs with us."

"But where?" Sami said, peering into the darkness.

Her echoing voice sounded like it was right next to the other side of the room, all at the same time. Then, just like that, the mysterious voice disappeared.

MJ looked down and picked up the leotard. "There's something in here," she noticed and began unwrapping the stretchy pink cloth. Inside, she discovered a peculiar box made of wood with gorgeous squiggly patterns and holes on all sides "It doesn't seem like there's a way to open it," MJ said, passing it to Eddie. He turned the box around in his hands but couldn't make sense of it either.

"What was the Ballerina trying to say to us?" Sami said, repeating her words. "The cashier needs a pen! Who is the cashier? *What kind of pen are we supposed to give them?*"

Eddie whipped out the AEB and started flipping through the pages. The kids had been underground so long that their eyes had adjusted to the light.

"There!" MJ shouted, reading over Eddie's shoulder. "Cashier is from the French word *caisse*, which means 'money box.'"

Eddie's eyes bugged out. "Treasure!" he exclaimed, shaking the little box.

Now it was Sami's turn with the AEB. He carefully opened the book to the section for words starting with P and started scanning the pages. "*Voilà!* Here it is," he said, pointing down at the entry for the word *pen*. "It comes from an Old French word as well," Sami said excitedly. "It means 'feather!'"

"Like one of those old-timey feather pens!" Eddie said. "But where are we going to find one of those down here?" he asked, looking around the damp catacombs. Everything went eerily quiet for a minute. The tour group had gone farther into the underground maze of the catacombs, and all the kids could hear now was the steady dripping of water.

Then suddenly, the AEB fell out of Sami's hands. Actually it felt to Sami like it jumped from his hands. When the three friends looked down, they couldn't believe what they saw right there in the pages of the old book.

"A feather!" MJ exclaimed.

"I wonder if it was left in there by my great-grandpa Oscar when he was writing the book," Eddie whispered. He picked up the feather and brushed it against the box and waited. Nothing happened.

But then MJ noticed a small hole in the front of the box. "Try poking that hole with the tip of the

feather," she suggested.

Eddie turned the feather pen around and slowly pushed the pointy end into the tiny hole. "Something's happening!" he shouted. Eddie could feel gears churning inside the box. Slowly the peculiar box opened and revealed its contents.

"More movies?" MJ groaned. There were three red tickets in the box.

"These are no movie tickets," Sami said excitedly. "These are tickets to the Louvre Museum for the opening of its *Bastet Cat* exhibit"—he picked

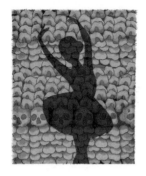 them up to get a closer look—"which starts in only one hour!"

Just then, out of the corner of his eye, Sami saw the Ballerina's shadow dart across the wall. "Catch me if you can!" They heard her voice echoing through the catacombs.

The three friends gave chase. They sprinted through the maze of the catacombs following the Ballerina's shadow. Eddie's head was spinning. "She's everywhere and nowhere at the same time!" he said. They kept going farther and farther into the depths of the underground tomb.

Sami gave Eddie a concerned look. "If we don't find a way out, we're going to be stuck down here for a very long time."

"There!" MJ said. She had caught a glimpse of the Ballerina's shoe. "She's gone into that dark tunnel."

"Are you sure about this?" Eddie asked MJ.

"Trust me!" MJ replied as she crouched down on the ground. The tunnel zigged and then it zagged before zigging yet again. It went on like that for a long while, when suddenly Eddie noticed a light in the distance.

"Keep going!" he shouted.

MJ, Eddie, and Sami began crawling through the tunnel at double speed. The light got bigger until, all at once, they tumbled out the other side of a sewer drain. They had been in the darkness of the catacombs for so long that the afternoon light was blinding. But when their eyes adjusted, they were amazed at what they saw.

"Pyramids?!" MJ and Eddie said at exactly the same time.

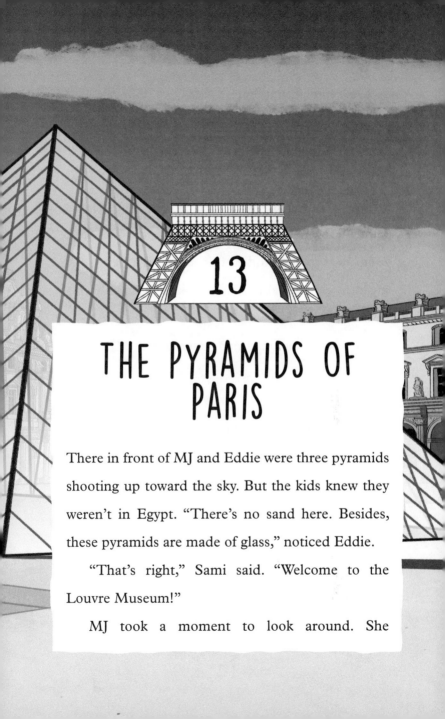

THE PYRAMIDS OF PARIS

There in front of MJ and Eddie were three pyramids shooting up toward the sky. But the kids knew they weren't in Egypt. "There's no sand here. Besides, these pyramids are made of glass," noticed Eddie.

"That's right," Sami said. "Welcome to the Louvre Museum!"

MJ took a moment to look around. She

remembered from Ms. Cassatt's art class that the Louvre Museum is home to many famous paintings like the Mona Lisa. *What an oddly beautiful place*, she thought to herself. They were standing in the massive courtyard of the museum, surrounded by an elegant old building that looked almost like a castle. But right there in the middle of the courtyard were three gigantic glass pyramids that looked like something out of an alien movie.

A snooty-looking man interrupted MJ's day-dream. "Tickets, please. This is a private event," he snarled.

Sami reached into his pocket and pulled out three tickets for the *Bastet Cat* exhibit. "Here you go, sir," the boy said with a smirk.

The man scowled and showed them into the museum through the doors in the glass pyramid. The event was already in full swing, and the gallery was packed with people. In the center of the room, a crowd had gathered around a glass case. As the threesome pushed through the fancy crowd of **elite** Parisians to get a closer look, MJ noticed two men in stripy suits standing at the other end of the gallery.

"The Raffles Brothers!" she shouted to the others. "They're watching over the soon-to-be-theirs Bastet Cat, I guess."

Finally, the kids got close enough to the glass case to see what all the commotion was about. The Bastet Cat was unlike any ancient Egyptian artifact any of them had ever seen. The life-sized cat statue was painted with brilliant blues, oranges, and yellows. Since it had been lost in the Louvre's vaults for many years, the artifact was in perfect shape.

Eddie picked up a **brochure** and read aloud. "In ancient Egypt, cats were held in high regard and even worshiped for more than three thousand years," he began.

But suddenly the lights went out in the gallery. The partygoers started to panic, confused by what was happening. "Calm down, everyone!" the snooty

guard said. "There must be a blown fuse." With that, he hurried off, flashlight in hand.

After a few minutes, the lights came back on, and the jazz music started back up. For a moment, everything went back to normal. When suddenly, the silhouette of the Ballerina flashed across the gallery wall, Sami jumped into action doing his parkour tricks, bouncing and flipping around the room. But it was no use.

GASP!

OH MY!

IT CAN'T BE…

Eddie, MJ, and Sami ran back toward the glass case. MJ was almost afraid to look. "It's gone! Right from under our noses too," she said. A perfect circle had been cut into the glass, and the statue had been expertly removed.

The Raffles Brothers were angrily complaining to the museum curator. "Something must be done," they pleaded. "The Bastet Cat is rightfully ours!"

Then, MJ noticed something on the pedestal where the cat had just been. "An Eiffel Tower souvenir," she said, picking up the cheap knickknack. "The Ballerina sure has a sense of humor."

"We were being played like a fiddle all along," Eddie said. "The Ballerina was toying with us just to get her kicks. In the end, she took the priceless artifact from right under our noses."

"I'd better let Mr. Pierre at the *Journal* know," MJ said, turning around to leave. "What were we thinking? We're not reporters."

"Wait!" said Sami. He turned over the souvenir. There was a small piece of paper glued to the bottom, with a bunch of colorful dots. "What's this?"

MJ remembered what Ms. Cassatt showed the kids on their class trip. "Pointillism!" she exclaimed. "I'll hold this up and you two walk backward."

As Eddie and Sami stepped backwards, the dots revealed a message!

Rendezvous at two
In Eiffel's **hotel** room
With a **magnificent** view
Be careful to **parachute**

"She wants to meet at two o'clock," Sami said, looking up at the others. "That first French word. You may know it," he said, then pronounced the word slowly: "*RON-DAY-VOO...*"

"That means when you plan to meet up somewhere in secret, right?!" Eddie shouted.

"Exactly," Sami replied. "The trouble is, Gustave Eiffel is famous for his tower, but I've never heard anything about a hotel."

"Hmm...according to the AEB, the original meaning of hotel is French for any kind of home or lodging," MJ offered. She had flipped open the book as soon as a new clue from the Ballerina appeared.

"A home or apartment with a magnificent view," Eddie considered. "It must be up high somewhere."

"Right! Look at the last line," Sami said, pointing down. "Be careful to parachute."

"I'm not parachuting anywhere!" Eddie said. He was more than a little scared of heights.

"There's got to be something else," MJ said,

ignoring Eddie's antics. She threw him the AEB. "Here!" she shouted.

Eddie jumped into action, flipping through his great-grandfather's old book. By now, he could almost feel his way to the right page. "P is for ptero-dactyl. No! Too far." He flipped backwards until he found the entry. "There! Parachute," he announced. "Parachute comes from the French *para-*, meaning 'protect,' and *chute* meaning 'fall.'"

The kids looked back down at the clue. "The Ballerina is telling us to be careful because we're going up something really tall..." MJ whispered.

"Gustave Eiffel's secret apartment..." Sami added.

All three kids looked down at the chintzy souvenir as it dawned on them.

"At the top of the Eiffel Tower!" MJ, Eddie, and Sami said all at once.

EIFFEL'S SECRET APARTMENT

Sami and the other kids jumped into a car with a glowing green sign on its roof that read *TAXI* in big black letters.

"To the Eiffel Tower!" Eddie told the driver.

Just like that, the taxicab took off through the streets of Paris. When the taxi screeched to a halt, MJ looked up and realized they were in front of the famous landmark. "It looks way bigger when it's right here in front of you," MJ said, looking up with her hands above her eyes.

"Quick! The elevator to the top is coming. Let's go!" Sami announced. The three friends filed onto a big elevator with glass windows. There were lots of thuds and clunks and sounds of gears turning. Then the elevator slowly came to life. As they climbed higher, the view of Paris just got better and better.

"You know what the only thing better than a view of the Eiffel Tower is?" MJ asked. But everyone was too busy looking out the window. *A view from the Eiffel Tower*, she said to herself.

Finally, when they reached the top, the elevator clunked to a stop. All of the other tourists got out and turned to the right. "There!" Eddie spied a door in the other direction. It had no markings.

The trio stood in front of the door nervously. MJ knocked twice. Nothing happened. Then, without warning, the door creaked open. A brunette wearing a pink ballet outfit peeked out and motioned for the kids to enter.

"Come in," she said. "I've been waiting for you."

"Where is the Bastet Cat?!" Eddie snarled. He was in no mood to play games.

"Wait! It's not what you think," the Ballerina shouted, waving her hands in the air.

Sami looked around and saw a tiny but beautifully designed little apartment, right there at the top of the Eiffel Tower.

"This was Gustave Eiffel's real-life secret apartment," the Ballerina explained. "After he became world-famous for designing the tower, he used this place to host people like the inventor of the light bulb, Thomas Edison."

"Whoa," MJ whispered as the three friends sat down.

"With the Raffles Brothers hot on our trail, I thought Eiffel's secret apartment would be the safest place to meet with you and explain everything," said the Ballerina.

"One thing's for sure. You have a lot of explaining to do," MJ replied.

The Ballerina sat down in an old armchair. "You see, after I decided to retire from my 'job' as an art thief, I became bored. I missed the thrill of the chase," she began. "But as I grew older, I began to change too. I started to realize that stealing priceless art for my own collection was selfish. Art should be shared with the world…"

"Yes!" Sami exclaimed.

"So when I decided to make my return," the Ballerina continued, "I wanted to correct my past mistakes and do something good for the art world."

"That's why you stole a priceless Egyptian artifact?" Eddie said, not believing the Ballerina's story.

"Hear her out, Eddie," said MJ. "Why would she have brought us all the way up here, even after she had the Bastet Cat?"

The Ballerina smiled at MJ. "The Bastet Cat does

not belong to those dastardly Raffles Brothers, who would have kept it for their own enjoyment only."

"That's right," Eddie said.

"And it's not even for the Louvre Museum!" she said. "This beautiful ancient artifact belongs to the people of Egypt, where it was originally taken from."

Sami's eyes started watering up. "You took the Bastet Cat statue so you could bring it back to its rightful home in Egypt. That's wonderful!" he said, thinking about all the times his father told him about Egyptian artifacts that had been taken to other countries.

"Now, I just need your help one more time," the Ballerina whispered, looking at MJ and Eddie. The two friends nodded. "Please talk to the curator of the Louvre Museum and see if we can't have a replica of the cat made for visitors to enjoy," she asked.

Eddie had a wonderful idea. "Sami's dad can make it for us!" he shouted.

"He's always wanted to have his work shown in

the museums of Paris," Sami replied.

"And I'll get to writing our story for the *Journal*. I think I have the perfect title," MJ said looking out over the City of Lights. "'Ballerina Cleans Up Her Act and Brings Bastet Cat Back.'"

With that, the AEB spilled out of Eddie's backpack and began spinning faster and faster in the air. Eddie and MJ held on tight to their chairs as the room filled with smoke.

"**Bon voyage**!" They heard Sami shout.

POOF!

In the blink of an eye, the two best friends were stepping off the school bus at the bottom of Magnolia Street where they both lived.

"That sure was an *extraordinary* class trip to the art museum," MJ said, smiling at her friend. Like all of their adventures, it all felt like a dream at first. But then, as Eddie and MJ moseyed up Magnolia Street toward their houses, something amazing happened.

"Look who it is!" MJ pointed down at the ground.

A stray kitten had appeared out of nowhere and was purring at her feet.

"It's our little pal from Paris," Eddie exclaimed, looking down at the kitty. "I think she wants us to bring her home. What should we call her?"

The two looked at each other and thought for a moment. "Bastet!" they shouted at once.

MJ crouched down and picked up the stray kitty. "C'mon, Bastet, let's go home and get you something to eat!"

GLOSSARY

baguette

(n.) ba-ˈget

A long, thin type of bread. In French, the word
literally translates to "wand, rod or stick."

beret

(n.) bə-ˈrā

A round, flat woolen hat originally worn by
peasants from the Basque region on the border of
France and Spain. It comes from the French word
béret meaning, "cap."

bon voyage

(n.) bän- vwä-ˈyäzh

A way to wish someone good luck before they depart on a journey. It comes from the French phrase which translates to "good journey."

brochure

(n.) brō-ˈshūr

A small book or magazine which contains written information and often has pictures. It comes from the French word, *brocher* which means "to stitch" (sheets together).

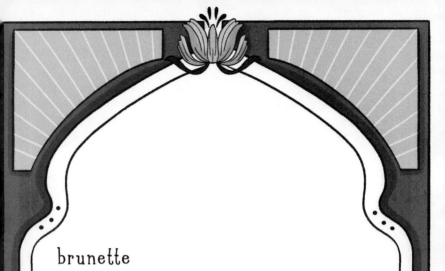

brunette

(adj.) brü-ˈnet

A woman with dark hair. It comes from the Old French word *burnete* which means, "a dark brown cloth made of wool."

café

(n.) ka-ˈfā

A coffee-house or restaurant. It comes from the French *café* which means coffee.

THE KNIFE AND STICK CAFÉ

canvas

(n.) ˈkan-vəs

A cloth made from a sturdy material called hemp. Originally from the Old French word *chanevaz* meaning "made of hemp."

cashier

(n.) (ˌ)ka-ˈshir

A person in charge of money. It is from the French word *caissier* which means, "treasurer" and *caisse* which translates to "money box."

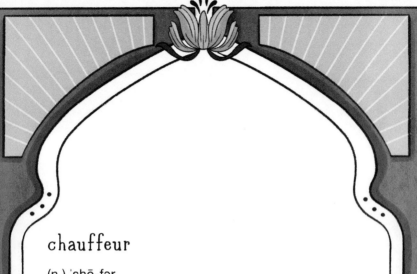

chauffeur

(n.) ˈshō-fər

Someone who drives others in a private or rented car. It comes from the French word which means someone who operates a steam engine. Some of the first cars were powered by steam engines.

cinema

(n.) ˈsi-nə-mə

A place to watch movies. It is from the French word *cinéma* shortened from *cinématographe* which describes a projector that shows a series of photos which would create the illusion of movement like a flip book.

141

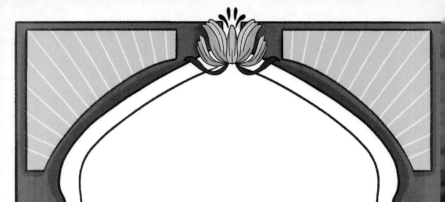

crayon

(n.) ˈkrā-ˌän

A colored wax used for writing or drawing. From the French word *crayon*, which comes from an earlier word, *craie*, meaning "chalk" or "clay."

debris

(n.) də-ˈbrē

A bunch of rubbish or scattered pieces left after something has been destroyed. From the French word *débris* meaning, "waste or rubbish."

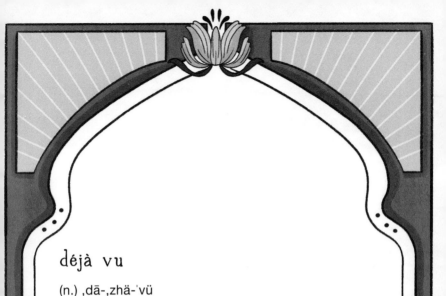

déjà vu

(n.) ˌdā-ˌzhä-ˈvü

The strange and awesome feeling of having already experienced a situation. It comes from the French word, *déjà vu* which means "already seen."

detour

(n.) ˈdē-ˌtūr

An alternate road, route or roundabout way to get somewhere. It comes from the French word *détour* which means "side road."

elite

(n.) ā-ˈlēt

A group of people or things that are the very best. It comes from the Old French word *eslite*, which means, "pick out or choose."

en route

(adv.) än-ˈrüt

A French phrase which literally translates to "on the way."

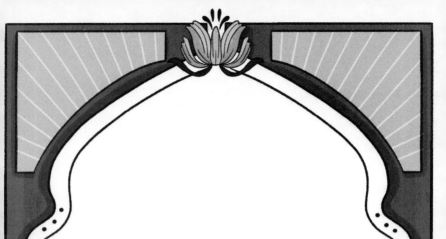

fountain

(n.) ˈfaün-tən

Meaning a spring of water that collects in a pool. It is from the Old French word *fontaine* which means "natural spring."

foyer

(n.) ˈfȯi(-ə)r

An entrance or open area often times in a hotel or theater. It comes from the French word which was used to describe a room for actors when they weren't on the stage.

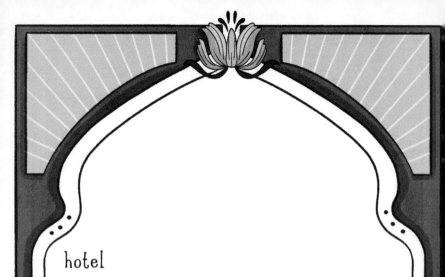

hotel

(n.) hō-ˈtel

An establishment that provides a place to sleep for travelers. It comes from the French word *hôtel* which means, "a mansion, palace or large house."

journal

(n.) ˈjər-nəl

A personal diary, newspaper or magazine. From the French word *journal* which means "that which takes place daily."

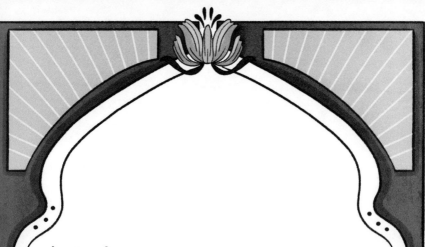

leotard

(n.) ˈlē-ə-ˈtärd

A stretchy one-piece article of clothing often worn by dancers or people exercising. It was created and made popular by the French trapeze artist, Jules Léotard (1830-1870), which is where it got its name.

magnificent

(adj.) mag-ˈni-fə-sənt

Something that is very grand or beautiful. From the Old French word meaning, "glorious actions or deeds."

marvelous

(adj.) ˈmärv-(ə-)ləs

Causing wonder or amazement. From the old French word, *merveillos* meaning, "wonderful."

matinee

(n.) ˌma-tə-ˈnā

An afternoon performance or entertainment that happens during the day. It comes from the French word *matin*, which means "morning."

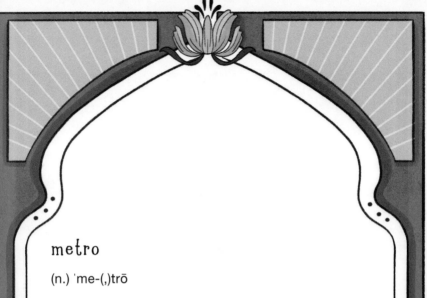

metro

(n.) ˈme-(ˌ)trō

A railway or form of public transportation. It comes from the French abbreviation of *Chemin de Fer Métropolitain* which means, "Metropolitan Railway" and was the company that built Paris' first subway lines.

omelet

(n.) ˈäm-lət

A dish that is made of beaten eggs mixed with other ingredients. From the French word *alemette* which means "thin, knife blade," referring to the shape of this breakfast food.

on point

(adj.) ˈȯn ˈpȯint

Excellent; bold or performing well. The exact origin
of the phrase is unknown. Possibly from the French
en pointe meaning, "to be on the tip of the toes in
ballet, reflecting a higher degree of skill."

palette

(n.) ˈpa-lət

A flat surface which is used by artists to mix colors.
From the Old French word, *palete* which means,
"small shovel or blade."

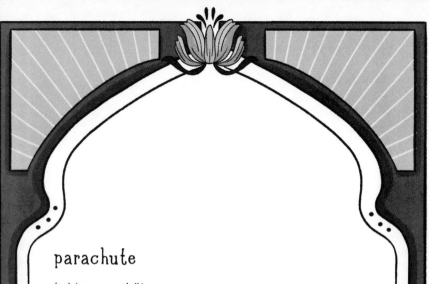

parachute

(n.) ˈper-ə-ˌshüt

A thin cloth that opens up like an umbrella to slow the fall of someone jumping from an airplane. The first parachute was used in Paris in 1784. The term was coined by French aeronaut, François Blanchard (1753-1809) from *para-* "defense against" and *-chute* "fall."

pencil

(n.) ˈpen(t)-səl

An object that you write or draw with. It comes from the French word *pencil*, which means an artist's small, fine brush of camel hair.

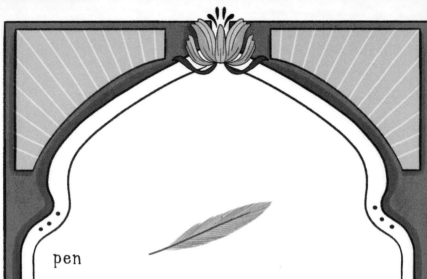

pen

(n.) ˈpen

A tool used for writing or drawing with ink. It comes from the French word meaning, "long feather of a bird."

plaque

(n.) ˈplak

A flat plate, usually made of metal, with writing and decoration on it. It comes from the French word which means metal plate or coin.

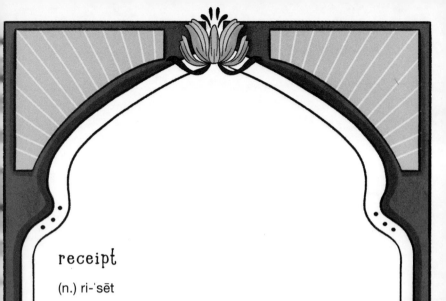

receipt

(n.) ri-ˈsēt

A piece of paper showing a list of items received and if money was exchanged. It comes from the French word, *receit* which means, "a list of ingredients or instructions to make a potion or medicine."

rendezvous

(n.) ˈrän-di-ˌvü

A word to describe assembling friends or setting up a date. It is from the French word, *rendez-vous* which translates to "present yourselves."

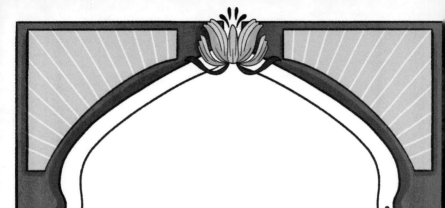

reporter

(n.) ri-ˈpȯr-tər

A person who reports stories or events to keep the public updated. It comes from the French word *reporteur*, which means to talk about what someone else said or did.

reservoir

(n.) ˈre-zə-ˌvwär

A place where water or another liquid collects. It comes from the French *réservoir* which means, "storehouse."

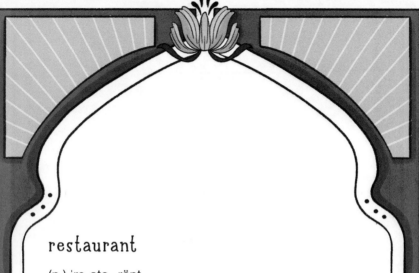

restaurant

(n.) ˈre-stə-ˌränt

A place people go to buy and eat meals. It is from the French word *restaurer* which means, "to restore or refresh."

silhouette

(n.) ˌsi-lə-ˈwet

A picture of a person or object, filled in with a single color. Named for a French politician, Étienne de Silhouette, who was very stingy. His name may have started being used as a slang term for "shadow paintings"—a cheap style of making portraits by tracing a person's shadow.

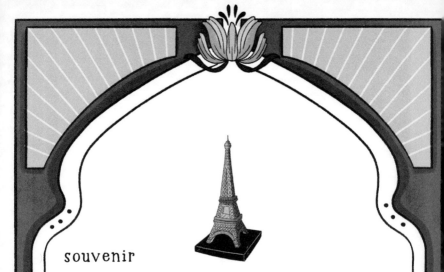

souvenir

(n.) ˈsü-və-ˌnir

Something you keep as a reminder of a place, event or friendship. It comes from the French word *souvenir* which means "something you remember, or a memory."

sport

(n.) ˈspȯrt

An activity that offers amusement or relaxation; entertainment or fun. It comes from the Old French word *desporter* meaning to seek amusement or literally "carry away" your mind from serious matters.

toilet

(n.) ˈtȯi-lət

Originally from the French word, *toilette* meaning "cloth" referring to the clothing you get dressed in. Later, the meaning transformed to a dressing room with a bathroom attached to it.

ABOUT THE AUTHOR

Raj Haldar must like words a lot. Under his alter ego, Lushlife, the rapper and multi-instrumentalist, he's spent close to a decade fitting words together into remarkable rhymes for fans all over the world. So it should come as no surprise that Raj's children's books are all about words too. His first picture book series, which includes *P Is for Pterodactyl*, was an instant smash with word nerds of all ages who love having fun with silent letters, homonyms, and other hilariously confusing parts of the English language. Now, with the Word Travelers series, Raj is introducing kids to the fascinating world of etymology and word origins, following his heroes, Eddie and Molly-Jean, on their globe-trotting adventures as they discover how common words came into the English language from cultures around the world. He lives on the Upper West Side of Manhattan with his wife and two young daughters.

ABOUT THE ILLUSTRATOR

Beatriz Castro is a professional illustrator. Growing up in Logroño, La Rioja, Spain, she was inspired by the natural world around her, to draw and write fantastic stories. She is passionate about animals and books, and enjoys traveling when she can. She lives with her husband and their three dogs, León, Greta, and Loba.